NOODLEHEADS FORTRESS OF DOOM

by Tedd Arnold
Martha Hamilton
and Mitch Weiss

illustrated by Tedd Arnold

HOLIDAY HOUSE · NEW YORK

To the young reader who finished
our first few Noodlehead books
and asked if there were any more.
This one's for you, Calvin!
—Tedd, Martha, and Mitch

Text copyright © 2019 by Tedd Arnold, Martha Hamilton, and Mitch Weiss
Illustrations copyright © 2019 by Tedd Arnold
All Rights Reserved
HOLIDAY HOUSE is registered at the U.S. Patent and Trademark Office.
Printed and bound in November 2020 at Toppan Leefung, DongGuan City, China.
The artwork was rendered digitally using Photoshop software.
www.holidayhouse.com
3 5 7 9 10 8 6 4 2

Library of Congress Cataloging-in-Publication Data:

Names: Arnold, Tedd, author, illustrator. | Hamilton, Martha, author. | Weiss, Mitch, 1951– author.
Title: Noodleheads Fortress of Doom / by Tedd Arnold, Martha Hamilton, and Mitch Weiss ; illustrated
by Tedd Arnold.
Other titles; Fortress of Doom
Description: First edition. | New York : Holiday House, [2019] | Series: Noodleheads; 4 | Summary:
Using knowledge from a library book, brothers Mac and Mac build a fortress but Meatball, armed with
a book of his own, wants to take it from them.
Identifiers: LCCN 2019006111 | ISBN 9780823440016 (hardcover)
Subjects: | CYAC: Fools and jesters—Fiction. | Books and reading—Fiction. | Building—Fiction.
Brothers—Fiction. | Humorous stories. | BISAC: JUVENILE FICTION / Readers / Intermediate
Classification: LCC PZ7.A7379 Nrm 2019 | DDC [E]—dc23
LC record available at https://lccn.loc.gov/2019006111

ISBN: 978-0-8234-4001-6 (hardcover)
ISBN: 978-0-8234-4837-1 (paperback)

NOODLEHEADS
FORTRESS OF DOOM

CHAPTER 1

IF WE BUILD IT...

My book is all about the Fortress of Doom!

Hey, Mac, what's all this wood in our backyard?

NOODLEHEADS FORTRESS OF DOOM

CHAPTER 2
GUARDING THE DOOR

Minutes later...

I got the snacks, Mac.

Great!

Huh?

What are you doing way over **there?**

I followed a really **cool** butterfly. Come see!

But you are supposed to be guarding the door to the fortress.

I am guarding the door!

But the fortress is way over **there.**

And I'm guarding the door **here.**

It's safely hidden behind this bush.

NOODLEHEADS FORTRESS OF DOOM

CHAPTER 3
TAKING THE FORTRESS

Wait! I dropped my book inside your fortress.

That's too **easy!**

We're even better at **tall tales!**

Listen up! After I was a baby, I grew so **tall...**

...my blanket didn't cover my feet anymore.

To make it longer, I cut off the top half of my blanket...

...and sewed it on the **bottom** to cover my feet!

And the best part was that I did it to **my** blanket too!

Good **tall** tale, right? We **win!** Go home now, Meatball!

Bye!

That story was so-o-o-o boring, even my **feet** went to sleep.

My turn. One time I survived a bad, **bad** storm.

It rained so much, the creek began to rise.

That creek rose so high I could walk **under** it!

The wind was **bad** too. I saw a hen lay an egg...

...and the wind blew that egg right **back** in her!

I started to laugh at that poor chicken. Just then, a fish...

...fell from the bottom of the creek, right into my **mouth!**

I **swallowed** it. It was swimming around in me.

That's **awful!** Is it still in there?

No. My dad got his fishing pole, dropped a line down my throat, caught that fish, and **cooked** it for dinner!

Now, **that,** my friends, is a real tall tale!

But there's nothing **tall** in your tale. The hen isn't tall.

The fish isn't tall. And you aren't tall!

And besides, our story is **true.** You made yours up.

Oh, **there** you are. What have you two been doing all day?

We've been building...

MY GARDEN SHED!

This wood was for my new **garden shed!**

Actually, this isn't so bad, if I just...

...move this board... straighten this...

...cut this board...

SAW SAW

...paint this...

WHAM

WHAM

Authors' Notes

Story Sources for *Noodleheads Fortress of Doom*

Tales of fools, also called "noodles" or "noodleheads," have been told for as long as people have told stories. In 1888, W. A. Clouston wrote a scholarly book called *The Book of Noodles* in which he described numerous stories that had been told for hundreds of years, with quite a few dating back over two millennia. We have used these old stories as inspiration for Mac and Mac's adventures.

Everyone has done something foolish. Here is one of many stories that Mitch and Martha could tell. In 1999, they were nearing the end of a five-hour drive home when they heard a news report on the radio about Yo-Yo Ma having left his cello in a taxi in New York City. They suddenly remembered that their laptop was still in the principal's office at the school where they had worked that week; they had stored it there so it would not sit in their hot car. Noodleheads! It took a good amount of money to ship it home safely. The only thing that made them feel better was that one of their heroes had done something far more foolish—left his rare, treasured cello, which was worth millions of dollars, in the trunk of a cab. Fortunately, the cello was found before his evening concert and all was well—just as often happens in the old stories. In spite of their foolishness, things usually turn out fine in the end for noodleheads, perhaps because they are generally kind and well meaning. Children find comfort in the fact that a foolish mistake usually doesn't mean the end of the world. Even if Mac and Mac don't learn from their mistakes, children who read about their adventures do. Noodlehead stories also help them understand humor, logical thinking, and the importance of distinguishing between what's true and what's a lie. Children quickly see that they should not always believe what they hear, especially when the source is a bully like Meatball.

The motifs to which we refer in the information that follows are from *The Storyteller's Sourcebook: A Subject, Title, and Motif Index to Folklore Collections for Children* by Margaret Read MacDonald, first edition, (Detroit: Gale, 1982) and second edition by Margaret Read MacDonald and Brian W. Sturm (Detroit: Gale, 2001). Tale types are from *A Guide to Folktales in the English Language* by D. L. Ashliman (NY: Greenwood, 1987).

Chapter 1: If We Build It . . .

Jokes are a genre of folklore—the stories, beliefs, customs, and traditions of a culture community of people that are passed along by word of mouth. Although it possible that the idea of knock-knock jokes dates back to Shakespec, this joke form became popular among adults in the 1930s in the United States. Although their popularity has waxed and waned, knock-knock jokes are still popular today, but are primarily thought of as jokes for children.

Chapter 2: Guarding the Door

Inspiration for this chapter came from tale type 1009, *Guarding the Door by Carrying It Away,* which is known throughout Europe and the Middle East. A retelling by Martha and Mitch, "When Giufa Guarded the Goldsmith's Door," can be found in *Noodlehead Stories: World Tales Kids Can Read & Tell* (Atlanta: August House Publishers, 2000). Sources for that retelling included Clouston's *The Book of Noodles* and *Italian Folktales* by Italo Calvino (New York: Harcourt Brace, 1980). Another inspiration was "Who Will Close the Door?" which can be found in Martha and Mitch's book *Stories in My Pocket: Tales Kids Can Tell* (Golden, CO: Fulcrum Publishing, 1996). The tale type is 1351, *Silence Wager,* and the motif is J2511.0.3 *First to speak must close door.* The story originated in India and was eventually well known throughout Europe; a famous version is the Scottish ballad "Get Up and Bar the Door."

Chapter 3: Taking the Fortress

Tall tales—stories that are outrageous exaggerations or outright lies told as if they are true—have a long history. Meatball understands that the teller of tall tales lies for the fun of it, uses creativity and invention to make others laugh, and does not expect to be believed. Because people have a natural tendency to compete with or "one-up" one another when telling these stories, lying contests and Liars' Clubs were born. Even today, there are several official Liars' Contests still held throughout the world. The story about the creek rising and the wind blowing the egg back into the hen was inspired by the story "Rain and Mud" by the late Chuck Larkin, a master teller of tall tales. It can be found at www.chucklarkin.com/stories/Short_Tales.pdf. Both stories fit into the motif X1600 *Lies about weather and climate.* Mac and Mac's "brilliant" idea to cut off the bottom half of the blanket and sew it to the top in order to make it longer (J1978 *Quilt too short . . .*) falls under the broader category *Absurd Disregard of Facts.*